Milly
in the Hamptons

A PHOTOGRAPHIC SUMMER

By Rianna Shaikh

Legwork Team
Publishing
NEW YORK

Legwork Team Publishing
www.legworkteam.com
New York

Copyright © 2015 Rianna Shaikh

ISBN: 978-1-935905-59-2

First Edition: 11/02/2015

Printed in the United States of America
This book is printed on acid-free paper

Design by Vaiva Ulenas-Boertje

Dearest Reader,

Last summer, I traveled to Montauk and had quite a grand adventure. Along with my family and Rosa, we even met a movie director with a dog like Frankie!

This summer, I had a brand new adventure in the fanciest place you could imagine—the Hamptons! I even had to wear a big hat, and I got to meet some very beautiful horses in the Hampton Classic. But, I made sure to capture my journey with lots and lots of photographs just for you!

Wishing you, my dear friends, a wonderful read and a photographic summer.

My love to you always,
Milly S.

*O*nce upon a town, surrounded by storybook homes and harbors, lived Milly. Her enchanting home was lovely to behold, with beautiful flower gardens and colorful birds perching delicately on stone fountains.

After last summer's visit to Montauk, Milly's dad decided to buy a summer beach house in the Hamptons. Milly was filled to the brim with excitement and couldn't wait until it was time to go.

Milly was loved greatly by everyone she met. She had her dad's charming manner and her Mom's eloquent flair. She enjoyed bedtime stories of monkeys and tigers from Africa, and tea-time with her brother and sister.

Milly's siblings, Ferrie and Prince Fehren, spent their time reading stories and watching the many animals that migrated to their backyard in the summertime.

Milly's little brother Fehren had Cerebral Palsy. He didn't walk or talk just yet, but Milly found ways to include him in everything she did—even getting into trouble!

One early summer morning, Milly sat on her back veranda enjoying her breakfast, sipping her tea, and staring at her dad as he read his New York Times.

"Mere jaan, what's the matter?" inquired Dad.

"I'm reading a book on the Hamptons. I can't wait to go!" said Milly.

"Soon, mere jaan, soon!" Dad smiled.

When evening arrived, Milly was in the "angel room" getting ready for story time. This was a room in her home that had angels painted on the ceiling. Every Wednesday evening at approximately 8:30 p.m., Milly, her brother, and her sister, cuddled in the angel room and had their tea while Dad told them many stories of his well-traveled childhood.

As Milly, Ferrie, and little Prince Fehren listened attentively, Dad eagerly told the children a story of his childhood travels to Africa. Dad's stories were so intriguing and often felt so real that Milly and her sister didn't want to go to sleep. But this time, as her dad went on and on, they soon fell fast asleep.

In the early morning, Milly's sister Ferrie went off to her last day of school at the Portledge. Ferrie loved the Portledge School and thought it was the best school ever. It reminded her of one of those exclusive boarding schools in Europe, but yet, here it was on Long Island. It looked like a sprawling chateau with acres and acres of land. Rumor has it that the principal is quite charming.

As Milly and Ferrie sat at their table with their dolls, their Mom made a scrumptious breakfast.

"Mom, when can we go to the Hamptons?" asked Milly. "It'll be so much fun."

"Oh honey, you are such a good salesperson, just like your Dad," smiled Mom.

As Mom turned away, Milly looked at Ferrie with a great big smile; "That's how it's done, Ferrie," as she took her dolls Beckah and Ellie upstairs.

As time would have it, it was decided that they would leave for their summer vacation that next morning. Milly knew this meant it was going to be a rather long night. Packing drove her Mom crazy.

Luckily, their greatly loved housekeeper, Rosa Lee, was going to be doing a lot of the packing that night. The girls knew that this would mean a lot of yelling and fussing because Milly and Ferrie were very particular about their clothing.

"Thank god for Rosa, Mom," smiled Milly. "She keeps me sane!"

Soon it was early morning, and Mr. Patel, their driver, stood in their driveway waiting…and waiting…waiting for everyone!

After half past nine, everyone had their things packed, and off they went to the Hamptons!

After two very long hours of driving they finally arrived in Southampton. Milly simply adored Southampton because of Tate's Bakeshop. It was the ultimate chocolate experience for her.

As Milly sat outside the bakery munching on chocolatey-chip cookies and sipping iced tea, she noticed all the women walking by with their hats and sundresses.

As Mr. Patel drove through the picturesque Main Street, they noticed many boutiques to shop in and places to sip tea and talk.

Milly was simply taken by the children riding their bikes with wicker baskets attached to the front of each bike, as they rode alongside their mothers.

Certainly, Milly thought, they looked like something out of a magazine.

Milly turned to her dad and thanked him for taking them to the Hamptons.

"You're welcome, mere jaan," he replied, smiling at her.

Milly then looked at her Hamptons guidebook again and reminded her dad that she wanted to have a clambake on the beach with the "Best Clam Bakers in the Hamptons—the Splish Splash Bros." Certainly her dad needed to keep working on Wall Street to afford all these lovely things Milly wanted!

As Mr. Patel drove down a very long driveway, Milly could hear waves crashing and got a whiff of the ocean air.

"How magical! I have waited my whole life for this, Daddy!" Milly exclaimed, as she got out of the car.

"Milly, you are only nine," sighed Ferrie.

Everyone smiled as they took their suitcases into the house.

Their first Sunday in the Hamptons was quite exceptional. As Milly woke up, she was pleased to have breakfast in bed while looking at the ocean.

The day flew by and as the evening sun was setting, Ferrie, Milly, Fehren, and Rosa Lee were walking on the beach. The waves lapped over Milly's toes, and she remembered her last summer in Montauk with Lou and Frankie.

As they walked on the beach, Milly saw a rather odd-looking old man with a long, trimmed beard and strange overgrown hair that looked like a frizzy bird's nest. He was trimming the green hedges in his garden, and they almost looked like they were shaped like his beard!

The odd man waved, and Rosa Lee waved back.

"Well, what do you know, Rosa Lee? There's quite a character, all right!" smiled Milly.

"Miss Milly, your mom would want you to be kind," smiled Rosa Lee.

Milly had imagined that her new Hamptons neighbors would be elegant, charming, and wearing dotted bow ties. She never expected to see such a peculiar-looking person.

The first few days went by quickly. Milly ate her breakfast outside on the beach each day, watching the waves. She attempted to read her very first chapter book, "The Wind in the Willows," but she thought that writers should put paintings on every page of chapter books, or else she'd fall asleep.

As she looked up, the odd-looking man from next door was a few steps away.

"Hello, I am Sir Benaji, and this is Redfin, my dog."

"Hello there, I'm Milly."

"Just Milly? Plain and simple, without a dimple," smiled the old man.

"I'm afraid so, plain and simple, without a dimple Milly."

"What an interesting necklace! I lost a key just like that one on the beach last summer when I was directing my latest movie."

"You're a movie director! Get outta town!" smiled Milly. "Well not really, but you know what I mean…" and she laughed.

Sir Benaji told Rosa Lee and Milly stories about his latest movie, and they were thrilled.

Late night fell, and as Milly sat in bed, she held the key in her hand and thought of what Sir Benaji had said. She turned it over and looked at the back.

There was an "A" and a "B" on it engraved in script.

"Hmmm," thought Milly. "I wonder if…" but then she forgot all about Sir Benaji and the key as she promptly fell asleep. I'm sure that she was dreaming of rabbits in Mister McGregor's garden.

The next sunny day came in like waves, and as Milly ate breakfast sitting on the sand, she felt she needed to see Lou. After all, the key she wore around her neck was really his.

Late in the afternoon, Milly's family was having lemonade on the back porch when they spotted Sir Benaji walking his dog Redfin.

"Would you like to join us, Sir Benaji?" Dad called out.

"Thank you. I would indeed," he replied.

"I've heard from my daughter that you are a movie director. Is that what brought you to the Hamptons?"

"It is," Sir Benaji began. "But the one who really wanted to move out here was my wife, Annabelle."

"Can we meet her?" Milly asked, wondering if she was as odd-looking as Sir Benaji.

"No, I'm sorry. Annabelle passed away over a year ago," Sir Benaji replied.

Oh, Milly thought to herself. "A.B." could stand for Annabelle Benaji! She felt quite sad for Sir Benaji.

"Milly, I've been wanting to ask you a question about your key," Sir Benaji began. "I lost two keys like that two summers ago. Where did you find it?"

"My friend Lou gave it to me last summer. He found it on the shore somewhere in Montauk." Milly wondered if indeed this key belonged to Sir Benaji.

As the dark clouds scurried on by, she stood on her balcony, looking at the waves. Milly always wanted to do the right thing, but this time, what was the right thing to do? Would Lou be mad at her for giving away their treasure key?

The next morning, Milly begged her mom to let her visit Lou at his beach house.

When Milly and Rosa Lee arrived at Lou's, a woman opened the door.

"So sorry, Miss Milly, Lou's grandfather was suddenly ill and I'm afraid he's gone to Europe."

Rosa Lee extended their sympathies, and Milly left a note:

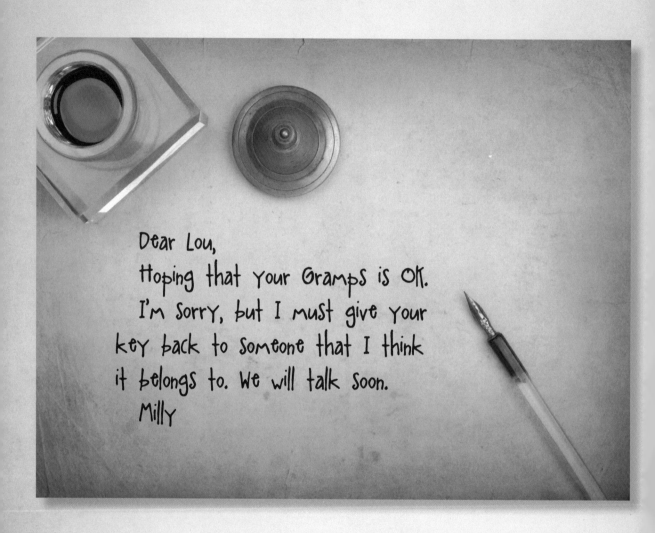

Dear Lou,
Hoping that your Gramps is OK.
I'm sorry, but I must give your
key back to someone that I think
it belongs to. We will talk soon.
Milly

Back at the beach house, everyone was getting ready for a clambake. As Milly walked into the kitchen, she poured her heart out to her mom. Her mom handed Milly an ice cream cone, and let's just say Milly totally forgot about her dilemma.

"Who's ready for a clambake?" Dad asked.

Milly and Ferrie yelled, "Me!"

As Milly walked out onto the sand, she saw yet another peculiar sight—the Splish Splash Bros. They were twin brothers with twin red mohawks, and they did the best clambake around.

Sir Benaji, in between eating his clams, had stories to share from here to Switzerland and back.

Rosa was in heaven sitting next to Sir Benaji; she thought a star from the sky had fallen on her. After all, he was famous!

As everyone finished their dinner, they returned to Milly's house for tea. In the garden room, Milly handed Sir Benaji the key.

"I think, Sir Benaji, that this is your key. It has initials on the back, A.B., for your wife Annabelle."

Sir Benaji reached out for the key and turned it over. Tears began to well up in his eyes.

"Milly, because you are so honest," said Sir Benaji, "I'll tell you the secret that this key holds."

As he invited everyone to his home, it was unlike anything she had ever imagined seeing.

As they all walked inside, they saw pictures on the wall of the famous people he knew. Over his stone fireplace was a portrait of his wife, Annabelle. She was quite beautiful.

They followed Sir Benaji to a hidden door behind a bookcase in his library. As he placed the key in the lock, the door squeaked open. It was a secret rose garden. There were vines of roses on the walls and fountains with statues of angels.

Everyone grew speechless, and Sir Benaji was filled with gratitude.

"I built this garden for my wife, and there are only two keys to this room. I had one, and Annabelle had the other. They both were lost after she died. I thought I might never be able to set foot into this room again."

"I'm so grateful that you returned the key, and as a thank you, I'd like to invite everyone to come with me to the Hampton Classic."

Surely it would be a day that Milly would never forget.

Late August arrived, and soon it was almost time to return to their other home in Upper Brookville. But before they were to leave, they were going to go with Sir Benaji to the Hampton Classic, one of the most prestigious horse shows in the world.

As Milly arrived at The Classic, she was impressed by all of the beautiful women in their big hats, and the beautiful horses.

Sir Benaji introduced Milly's family to the equestrians, which was such an honor!

After being acquainted with some of the most renowned horsemen in all of the world, Milly vowed to take Mrs. Eugene, her riding trainer, more seriously. So, when Mrs. E said, "No more horsing around!" Milly would surely listen.

In the essence of it all, it was time to bid au revoir to the Hamptons.

Milly certainly loved the Hamptons, from waking up to the sound of waves, to finishing her first chapter book, to returning the secret key to Sir Benaji.

Well, my Dad always says,
"Stick around, good things are ahead."
And that I did. Where did he think I was
going anyway?
To Africa, or Pakistan, or maybe Paris; but
I love America—especially Long Island.
With love,
Milly

Somewhere in Long Island it is written…

"To love the Hamptons, you gotta love the ocean breeze, clambakes, and Tate's Cookies." Milly certainly loved it all.

The End

My darlings,

I hadn't written for quite sometime, except for a children's tale, but I vow to do better. See, I've found a new love—writing novels for young ladies and gentlemen, and it's sure fun!

But I hadn't forgotten about you; no, that's an impossibility, and in life, there are few, if any. With your heart all in and your eyes glistening with hope, you can do anything!

However, I'm awaiting yet another story…maybe something in a secret garden with a little boy in a wheelchair, like my Prince Fehren. You can't forget him, as he's the light in my path of words and fountain pens…forever etched into my heart…and a writer without heart, isn't a writer.

May this and all of my books not only inspire my darlings Ferrie and Milly, but you, my dear readers. May you know that you do have my heart, always and forever.

Writing you a story, with the sunlight, and the stars at night…with of course, lots of tea!

From the Brookvilles,
Rianna Shaikh

Milly in the Hamptons

A PHOTOGRAPHIC SUMMER

For more information regarding Rianna Shaikh and her work,
visit her website: www.riannashaikh.com.

Additional copies of this book may be purchased online from
www.LegworkTeam.com; www.Amazon.com;
www.BarnesandNoble.com;
or via the author's website: www.riannashaikh.com.

You can also obtain a copy of the book
by ordering it from your favorite bookstore.

CPSIA information can be obtained at www.ICGtesting.com
Printed in the USA
BVIW12n0227181115
426320BV00001B/1